SCELIDOSAURUS
(ske-LI-doh-SAW-rus)

TYRANNOSAURUS
(tie-RAN-oh-SAW-rus)

TRICERATOPS
(try-SER-a-tops)

PTERODACTYL
(TER-oh-DAC-til)

STEGOSAURUS
(STEG-oh-SAW-rus)

APATOSAURUS
(a-PAT-o-SAW-rus)

ANCHISAURUS
(AN-ki-SAW-rus)

For Ella and Fifi and Teddy and Amelie with love.
You can sleep over with me and Nana any time – *I.W.*

For Jake – *A.R.*

PUFFIN BOOKS
Published by the Penguin Group: London, New York, Australia, Canada, India, Ireland, New Zealand and South Africa
Penguin Books Ltd, Registered Offices: 80 Strand, London WC2R 0RL, England

puffinbooks.com

First published 2010
1 3 5 7 9 10 8 6 4 2
Text copyright © Ian Whybrow, 2010
Illustrations copyright © Adrian Reynolds, 2010
Manufactured in China
Hardback ISBN: 978–0–141–32706–8
Paperback ISBN: 978–0–141–32707–5

Harry and the Dinosaurs
First Sleepover

Ian Whybrow 🐾 **Adrian Reynolds**

PUFFIN

Harry and the dinosaurs were helping to pack
his first sleepover bag.
Nan put in Harry's pyjamas, his washbag
and his clean clothes for the morning.

Harry put in his special box for his badges and shells,
his lucky light sabre, plenty of cars and robots,
plus a bedtime book and some moss for the dinosaurs.

Sam said they didn't need all that junk
and it was stupid putting moss in.

Harry said, "No, the moss is for the dinosaurs
to make sleeping bags if they want to."

He thought they might get scared and homesick
at his friend Jack's house.

Harry could tell that Mum and Nan were worried about leaving him. But Jack's mum and dad were nice and Jack showed him all the good places to hide in his house.

"Raaah! Seek me!" said Triceratops.

"Guess where I am!" said Scelidosaurus.

For a treat,
Jack's dad took them up the ladder into the attic
and showed them the bats sleeping.
He said they were a protected species, and nocturnal,
which meant they only flew in the night.

Harry asked if they would ever fly into your bedroom
and get stuck in your hair.
Jack's dad laughed and said, "Ha ha, not in my hair. Look!"

Dinosaurs can't always tell if dads are joking.
  "Why didn't he say that bats never get stuck
in little boys' hair?" they said.

Outside in the garden, Harry and Jack
had fun on the trampoline.
   The funniest part was when Triceratops
and Pterodactyl held hands with a robot
and did bouncing tricks with a Morris Minor.

Best of all, they played running in and out of
Jack's tent being cave men.
  The tent was great because it had a nice
mouldy smell to it.

Harry loved the soft way the tent rubbed the side
of your head when you stood up.

And Apatosaurus said, "Listen!" because you could
swish it with your tail and make it whistle.

That night they had extra bubbles in the bath.
And the dinosaurs had a good squirty fight with
Jack's bath toys.

"Raaah!" said the dinosaurs. "Big sharp teeth need extra brushing!"
  Then they all had fun squeezing tubes with different tastes.
  "Num num!" said Apatosaurus. "Leaf flavour! My favourite!"

Everyone thought sleepovers were excellent. They had three stories plus an extra five minutes for quiet play.

So they did puzzles and swapped cards. But the dinosaurs ended up making BLAAAAST noises with the robots. That was why Jack's mum came and told everybody to settle down.

Harry couldn't sleep at all, so Jack
stayed awake to keep him company.

"It's a bit dark,
even with the lucky light sabre on,"
said Stegosaurus.

The dinosaurs could hear something
going *tap-tap* on the window.
Stegosaurus was so nervous
he knocked Harry's special box on to the floor.

This time Jack's dad came upstairs and asked if everything was all right.

Harry said, "Yes. Only, a bat wants to come in through the window and it's a bit scary."

Jack's dad said not to worry,
        it was only leaves tapping,
                not bats, definitely.

Then he said, "I know something
that will make everyone feel really safe . . ."
And he ran downstairs and came back with Jack's tent.

It was lovely having a camp in the room,
with all the toys having special jobs to do.

There wasn't one beep out of the cars or the diggers.
Their job was to line up quietly in twos,
ready for some noisy action in the morning.

"We like guarding and blasting," whispered the robots.
  "Blaaaaast!"
  "Raaah!" said Pterodactyl quietly but firmly.
  "Stay outside, you bats!"
  "Hmmm, nice moss," murmured Stegosaurus.
His plates weren't rattling one bit.

"I like sleepovers," Harry whispered.
"I'm going to do lots and lots of them."

ENDOSAURUS

SCELIDOSAURUS

(ske-LI-doh-SAW-rus)

TYRANNOSAURUS

(tie-RAN-oh-SAW-rus)

TRICERATOPS

(try-SER-a-tops)

PTERODACTYL

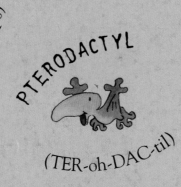

(TER-oh-DAC-til)

STEGOSAURUS

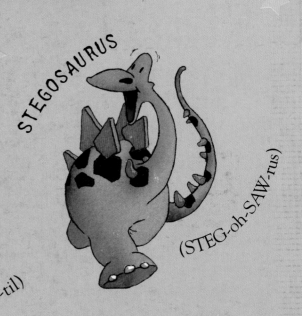

(STEG-oh-SAW-rus)

APATOSAURUS

(a-PAT-oh-SAW-rus)

ANCHISAURUS

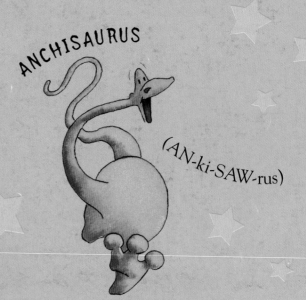

(AN-ki-SAW-rus)